What and Where

The Sound of WH

By Robert B. Noyed and Cynthia Klingel

The Child's World®, Inc.

What? Where? When? Why?

So many things are in the sky.

4

Where does the sun go at night?

What makes the sky blue?

8

When does lightning flash in the sky?

Why do the stars come out at night?

10

Where do rainbows end?

What makes the wind
blow?

16

When is the moon round and full?

Why do the clouds
make rain and snow?

20

Where? What? When?
Why?

So many things in
the sky.

Word List

what

when

where

why

Note to Parents and Educators

The books in the Phonics series of the Wonder Books are based on current research which supports the idea that our brains are pattern detectors rather than rules appliers. This means children learn to read easier when they are taught the familiar spelling patterns found in English. As children encounter more complex words, they have greater success in figuring out these words by using the spelling patterns.

Throughout the 35 books, the texts provide the reader with the opportunity to practice and apply knowledge of the sounds in natural language. The 10 books on the long and short vowels introduce the sounds using familiar onsets and rimes, or spelling patterns, for reinforcement. For example, the word "cat" might be used to present the short "a" sound, with the letter "c" being the onset and "-at" being the rime. This approach provides practice and reinforcement of the short "a" sound, as there are many familiar words made with the "-at" rime.

The 21 consonants and the 4 blends ("ch," "sh," "th," and "wh") use many of these same rimes. The letter(s) before the vowel in a word are considered the onset. Changing the onset allows the consonant books in the series to maintain the practice and reinforcement of the rimes. The repeated use of a word or phrase reinforces the target sound.

The number on the spine of each book facilitates arranging the books in the order that children acquire each sound. The books can also be arranged into groups of long vowels, short vowels, consonants, and blends. All the books in each grouping have their numbers printed in the same color on the spine. The books can be grouped and regrouped easily and quickly, depending on the teacher's needs.

The stories and accompanying photographs in this series are based on time-honored concepts in children's literature: Well-written, engaging texts and colorful, high-quality photographs combine to produce books that children want to read again and again.

Dr. Peg Ballard
Minnesota State University, Mankato

Photo Credits

All photos © copyright: Dembinsky Photo Associates: 7 (Stephen Graham), 8 (Adam Jones), 12 (Michael P. Gadomski), 19 (Mary Clay); Tony Stone Images: 3 (John Warden), 4 (Darryl Torckler), 11 (Don Spiro), 15 (John Callahan), 16 (Chad Ehlers); Unicorn: 20 (Joe Sohm). Cover: Dembinsky Photo Associates/ Richard Hamilton Smith.

Photo Research: Alice Flanagan
Design and production: Herman Adler Design Group

Library of Congress Cataloging-in-Publication Data

Noyed, Robert B.
    What and Where : the sound of "wh" / by Robert B. Noyed and Cynthia Klingel.
    p. cm. — (Wonder books)
    Summary: Simple text about the sky and repetition of the letters "wh" help readers learn how to use this sound.
    ISBN 1-56766-729-5 (alk. paper)
    [1. Sky Fiction. 2. Alphabet.] I. Klingel, Cynthia Fitterer. II. Title.
    III. Series: Wonder books (Chanhassen, Minn.)
    PZ7.N955Wh   1999
    [E]—dc21   99-15889
                                                       CIP